KODANSHA NIHONGO FOLKTALES SERIES 3

つるのおんがえし

THE GRATEFUL CRANE

KODANSHA INTERNATIONAL

Tokyo·New York·London

つる

むかし むかし、やま の なか に びんぼうな
おじいさん と おばあさん が すんでいました。
あるひ おじいさん が ゆき の なか を あるいて
いました。いちわ の つる が けが を して
ないて いました。おじいさん は つる を たすけて
あげました。
おじいさん 「かわいそうに。はやく うち へ かえりなさい」
つる 「おじいさん、ありがとう」
つる は うれしそうに とんで いきました。

5

おばあさん

おじいさん「おばあさん ただいま。

わたし は、きょう やまみち で、

つる を たすけて あげた よ」

おばあさん「まあ、いいこと を しました ね」

おじいさん「さあ、もう ねよう か」

そのとき そとで おと が しました。

とんとん とんとん

だれか が と を たたいて いました。

とんとん とんとん

6

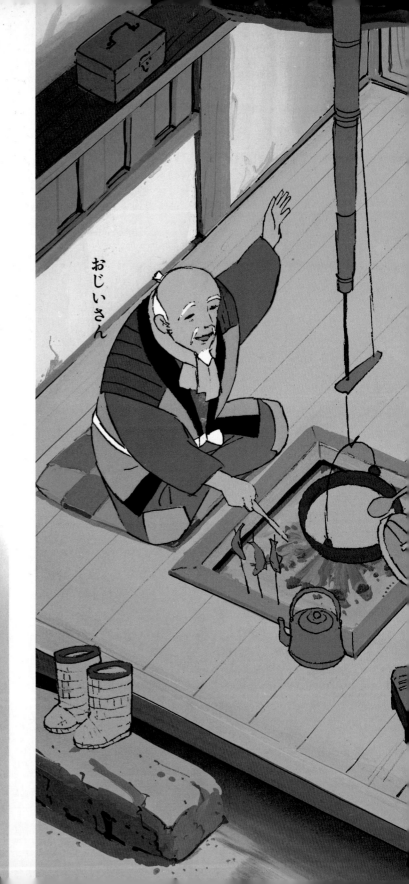

おばあさん　「だれでしょう、こんな　よなか　に。

だれ　が　きたのでしょう」

おじいさん　「はい　はい　いま　と　を

あけます　よ」

おじいさん

7

おじいさんがとをあけました。
そとにかわいいおんなのこが
たっていました。

おんなのこ　「こんばんは。わたし　の　へや　の　なか　を　あたたかく

なまえ　は　つう　です。

どうぞ　ひとばん　だけ　とめて　く

ださい。

おじいさん　「さむい　でしょう。

はやく　なか　に　はいりなさい」

おじいさん　と　おばあさん　は

して　あげました。あたたかい　おちゃ

も　いれて　あげました。

そして　みんなで　いろり　の

そば　で　ねました。

おじいさん　「おやすみ」

おばあさん　「おやすみ　なさい」

9

いろり

つぎ の あさ、つう は あさご
はん を つくりました。
あたたかい ごはん と みそしる
を つくりました。
つう 「おはよう ございます」
おじいさん 「おはよう」
おばあさん 「あさごはん つくって
くれた の?。 ほんとう に
おいしそう」
あさごはん の あと、つう は
つめたい みず で せんたく を
しました。 それから うちじゅう
の そうじ を しました。
おばあさん 「ねえ、わたしたちの
こども に なって ください よ」
おじいさん 「ここで いっしょに
くらして ください よ」
つう 「ええ、いっしょに くらし
ましょう」

10

いっしゅうかん たちました。

つう 「おじいさん と おばあ
さん の ために、はた
を おりたい の です。
はたおり の へや を
つくって ください。
おじいさん 「はい はい いい
です よ」
おじいさん は さっそく
ちいさな へや を つくり
ました。そこに、はたおり の
どうぐ と いと を おいて
あげました。
つう 「おじいさん おばあさん
わたし は こんや ひとばん
じゅう はた を おります。
でも、へや の なか を
みないで ください」

おじいさん と おばあさん

「わかりました よ」

つう 「やくそくです よ」

おじいさん と おばあさん

「はい はい」

つう は へやに

はいりました。やがて、

おと が きこえました。

♪ きっこ ぱた とん、

きっこ ぱた とん♪

ひとばんじゅう おと

が きこえました。

♪ きっこ ぱた とん、

きっこ ぱた とん♪

つぎのひ も

♪ きっこ ぱた とん、

きっこ ぱた とん♪

いと

ぬの

14

つぎの　ひ　の　あさ、
つう　は　へや　から
でて　きました。
つう　「おじいさん、でき
ましたよ。この　ぬの
を　うってきて　ください」
おじいさん　は　それ
を　みて、びっくり
しました。
おじいさん　「これ　は
すばらしい　ぬの　だ！」
おじいさん　は　その
うつくしい　ぬの　を
もって、まち　へ　うりに
いきました。

まちのひと

まち で おじいさん が
その ぬの を おおぜい
の ひと に みせました。
まちのひと一 「これ は
すばらしい ぬの だ!
わたし に じゅうりょう
で うって ください」
まちのひと2 「わたし に
にじゅうりょう で うって
ください」
まちのひと3 「わたし に
さんじゅうりょう で
うって ください」

とのさま も この
うつくしい ぬの を
みて びっくり
しました。

とのさま 「これ は
すばらしい つるのせん
ばおり だ。わたし に
ひゃくりょう で
うって くれ」

おじいさん 「えっ!
ひゃくりょう!」

おじいさん は
よろこんで ぬの
を ひゃくりょう で
うりました。

とのさま

おじいさん は おみやげ を たくさん かって うち へ かえりました。

おじいさん 「ただいま。あの ぬの を うってきた よ」

おばあさん 「おかえりなさい」

つう 「おかえりなさい」

おじいさん 「とのさま が ひゃく りょう で かって くださった のだよ」

おばあさん 「まあ、よかった です ね」

つう 「ほんとう に よかった です ね」

さんにん は ごちそう を たくさん つくって たべました。

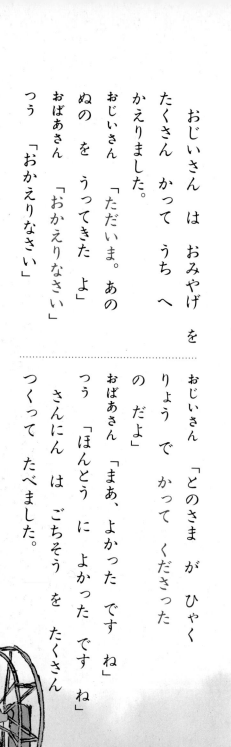

はたおり の どうぐ

つう「もう いちまい ぬの を おりましょう。けっして なか を みないで ください ね。やくそく ですよ」

つう は ひとばんじゅう おりつづけました。

♪ きっこ ぱた とん、
きっこ ぱた とん♪

つぎの ひも ひとばんじゅう おりつづけました。

♪ きっこ ぱた とん、
きっこ ぱた とん♪

おばあさん「どうして あんな うつくしい ぬの が できる のでしょう」

おじいさん「わからない。でも、みては

いけない よ」

おばあさん「ちょっと だけ みて きます」

おばあさん が へや の なか を みました。

やせた つる が はた を おって いました。むねの はね を ぬいて、はた を おって いました。

おばあさん「たいへんだ! たいへんだ! つる が はた を おっている」

つぎの ひ の あさ、つう は なきながら いいました。

つう 「もう ぬの を おること は できません」

おじいさん 「えっ、どうして！」

つう 「もう おわかれ しなければ なりません」

おばあさん 「えっ、どうして！」

つう 「わたし は ほんとう は つる です。

おじいさん に たすけて もらった……」

おじいさん 「ほんとう です。おんがえしに

つう 「えーっ、ほんとう です か！」

ここ へ きたの です」

おじいさん 「じゃあ どうして

つう 「わたし は つる です

おわかれ なの」

つう 「……

から……」

おばあさん 「つう、ごめんなさい。

ゆるして ちょうだい」

23

そのとき、つうは おおきな つる に なりました。

おばあさん 「つう、ゆるして ちょうだい。 いかないで」

おじいさん 「つう、まって くれ。 まって くれ」

つる 「さようなら さようなら」

つるは そらへ むかって なきながら とんで いきました。 いちど、にど、さんど、 わを かきながら とんで いきました。

おわり

25

★参考資料／野村純一・野村敬子編「雀の仇討」(東北出版企画)

すばらしい
Magnificent, wonderful.

p. 16
じゅうりょう
Ten *ryo*. *Ryo* was a kind of money used in feudal Japan, じゅう means ten.
じゅう—ten
にじゅう—twenty
さんじゅう—thirty
ひゃく—one hundred

ください
Would you...? See starred note on page ⑤ for a fuller explanation of ください.

にじゅうりょう
Twenty *ryo*.

さんじゅうりょう
Thirty *ryo*.

p. 17
とのさま
A kind of feudal lord.

つるのせんばおり
A magnificent and unique cloth. Literally, cloth woven with one thousand crane's feathers. Though this word is only used in this story, the word has become well-known in Japan.

ひゃくりょう
A hundred *ryo*.

うって くれ
Sell me.... This is not a polite way to ask someone to sell you something, but feudal lords didn't have to be polite! See starred note on page ⑤ for a fuller explanation of くれ.

p. 19
ただいま
I'm home, I'm back. This is what Japanese people say when they return home, for example, after a day's work, or a shopping trip.

おかえりなさい
This is the response to ただいま—Japanese people say it to welcome family home after they have been out. In English we would just say "Hello."

かって くださった
Was kind enough to buy. くださった is a less formal version of くださいました. See starred note on page ③ for a fuller explanation of くださいました.

p. 20
もう いちまい
Another piece. もう means another, and ₀₀₀まい is a way of counting flat objects such as cloth, stamps, records, paper, etc.

やせた
Thin.

はね
Feather.

たいへん
Goodness gracious me! This expression has several different meanings and is said when you are surprised or shocked.

p. 23
えっ
Eh?

しなければ なりません
We must.... To say "we must do something" in Japanese you add なければ なりません to the stem of the verb. For example, たべなけれが なりません— We must eat....

たすけて もらった
You helped me. もらった is a less formal way of saying もらいました. See starred note on page ③.

ゆるして ちょうだい
Please forgive me. See starred note on page ③ for a more detailed explanation of ちょうだい.

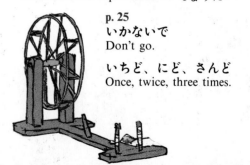

p. 25
いかないで
Don't go.

いちど、 にど、 さんど
Once, twice, three times.

おいしそう
It looks delicious.

うちじゅう
The entire house (from top to bottom). From うち, house and じゅう, the entire. じゅう is often added to other words to mean "the entire...."

ねえ
Listen. You can use this word when you start to say something, to make someone listen to you. It should not be used with people you do not know well.

★なって　ください
Please become, won't you become. ください is the most common way of asking someone to do something, and also the most useful, you can say it to anybody. Other, less polite ways are ちょうだい and くれ. For example:
みそしる　を　つくって　ください
Please make me some miso soup. Could you make me some miso soup.
みそしる　を　つくって　ちょうだい
Make me some miso soup, would you? (You can say this to a friend.)
みそしる　を　つくって　くれ
Make me some miso soup. (Not polite. Better not to use this.)

p. 12
いっしゅうかん
One week.

○○○の　ために
For.... As in おじいさん　の　ために—For you, Grandpa.

はた　を　おりたい　の　です
I want to do some weaving. Literally, I want to weave at a loom. From はた, loom, and おりたい, (I) want to weave.

はたおり　の　へや
A room for weaving.

おいて　あげました
Put, placed (for her). See starred note on page ③ for an explanation of あげました.

ひとばんじゅう
All night. Literally, the entire night. じゅう is often added to other words to mean "the entire...."

みないで　ください
Please don't look. See starred note on page ⑤ for an explanation of　ください.

p. 13
きっこ　ぱた　とん
Clackety clack clack. The noise made by the loom.

p. 15
うってきて　ください
Please go and sell.... Literally, please sell this and come back again. See starred note on page ⑤ for an explanation of ください.

まあ
My!

ね
Isn't it, wasn't it. A particle used in conversation to ensure that the listener is paying attention.

さあ
Well.

か
When placed at the end of a sentence, this particle turns the sentence into a question.

とんとん
Tap tap.

だれか
Someone. This word is made by adding か to だれ which means "who." か can be used to change the meaning of other question words in the same way. For example:

だれ who	だれか someone
どこ where	どこか someplace
なに what	なにか something
いつ when	いつか sometime

p. 7
はい　はい
Alright, alright, Literally, yes, yes.

p. 9
こんばんは
Good evening.

ひとばん
One night.

だけ
Just, only.

あたたかく　して　あげました
Warmed up for her, heated up for her. See starred note on page ③ for an explanation of あげました.

いれて　あげました
Made (some tea) for her.

いろり
Hearth.

おやすみ
Night, night. An informal way of saying "good night."

おやすみ　なさい
Good night. The addition of なさい makes this way of saying "good night" formal.

p. 10
あさごはん
Breakfast, morning meal. From あさ, morning, and ごはん, rice.

ごはん
Boiled rice, or a meal.

みそしる
Miso soup. Miso soup and rice make up the traditional Japanese breakfast, together with pickles, and sometimes fish.

おはよう　ございます
Good morning. This is the most formal way of saying "good morning."

おはよう
Morning. A less polite way to say "good morning."

つくって　くれた
Made for us. A less formal way of saying つくって くれました. See starred note on page ③.

④

Culture Notes

p. 1
つる
Crane. The crane is a symbol of long life, happiness and good health in East Asia, and appears in many Japanese folk tales. Another symbol of long life is the turtle. Traditionally, it is said that the crane lived for one thousand years and the turtle for ten thousand years.

おんがえし
Gratitude. More literally, the repaying of おん. おん in Japanese corresponds to something like the notion of indebtedness, but in a psychological rather than a monetary sense. It is often said to be more important in Japanese culture than in the West. You incur おん towards someone when they do something for you. You are then morally obliged to do something for them in return. For example, you have おん towards your parents for bringing you up. You may also have おん towards many other people who have done you favours—there is a Japanese saying that you incur おん through a single night's stay.

p. 5
びんぼうな
Poor.

おじいさん
Grandfather. Also has the wider meaning of "old man"—any old man, not just your own grandfather.

おばあさん
Grandmother. Similar to おじいさん、おばあさん has a wider meaning of "old woman."

いちわ
One bird. There are many different ways of counting in Japanese, depending on what you are counting.

けが を して
Injured.

★ **おじいさん は つる を たすけて あげました。**
The old man helped the crane. たすけて comes from たすける, which means "to help." あげました comes from あげる, which means "to give or do something for another person."
おじいさん は つる を たすけて くれました。
(or くださいました)
The old man helped the crane (for us). くれました comes from くれる, which means "to have something or some favor done by someone." If you are being very polite or the person who helped is a senior of yours, you use くださいました.

You can also use もらいました from もらう, which measns "to receive something or some favor from another person." as in おじいさん に つる を たすけて もらいました。"We had the old man help the crane for us."

かわいそうに
Poor thing!

ありがとう
Thank you. There are many ways of saying "thank you" in Japanese. This is one of the simplest and most generally useful.

うれしそうに
Happily. Literally, looking happy.

p. 6
あげた
Gave. Informal way of saying あげました. See starred note on page ③.

よ
…you see, …you know. A particle often placed at the end of a sentence to give it extra emphasis.

p. 15

On the morning of the following day, Tsuu came out of the room.

Tsuu: "Grandpa, I've finished. Please sell this cloth."

When the old man saw it, he was astonished.

Old man: "This cloth is magnificent!"

So the old man took the beautiful cloth and went into town to sell it.

p. 16

In the town, the old man showed the cloth to a large crowd of people.

Townsperson 1: "This cloth is magnificent! Would you sell it to me for ten *ryo*?"

Townsperson 2: "Would you sell it to me for twenty *ryo*?"

Townsperson 3: "Would you sell it to me for thirty *ryo*?"

p. 17

The lord of that place, too, was astonished when he saw the beautiful cloth.

Lord: "What a magnificent and unique piece of cloth. Sell it to me for one hundred *ryo*."

Old man: "Eh? One hundred *ryo*?"

So the old man happily sold the cloth for one hundred *ryo*.

p. 19

The old man bought lots of presents and went home.

Old man: "I'm home. I sold the cloth."

Old woman: "Hello."

Tsuu: "Hello."

Old man: "His lordship was kind enough to buy it for one hundred *ryo*."

Old woman: "My, that's good, isn't it?"

Tsuu: "That really is good, isn't it?"

Then the three of them made themselves a feast of delicious food.

p. 20

Tsuu: "I'll we

count must you look inside

alright?"

Tsuu wove all night.

— Clackety clack clack, clackety clack clack.

The next day, too, she wove all night.

— Clackety clack clack, clackety clack clack.

Old woman: "I wonder how she manages to make such beautiful cloth."

Old man: "I don't know. But we musn't look."

Old woman: "I'm just going to have a quick peek."

So the old woman looked inside the room. A thin crane was doing the weaving. She was weaving the cloth with feathers plucked from her own breast.

Old woman: "Goodness, gracious me! It's a crane doing the weaving."

p. 23

The next morning Tsuu spoke to them in tears.

Tsuu: "I can't weave any more cloth."

Old man: "Eh? Why?"

Tsuu: "I have to leave you now."

Old woman: "Eh? Why?"

Tsuu: "I am really a crane. Grandpa came to my rescue…"

Old man: "Eh? Is this true?"

Tsuu: "It's true. I came here out of gratitude, to repay you for your kindness."

Old man: "So why do you have to leave?"

Tsuu: "Because I'm a crane…"

p. 25

Old woman: "Tsuu, I'm sorry. Please forgive me."

But at that moment Tsuu turned into a large crane.

Old woman: "Tsuu, please forgive me. Don't go."

Old man: "Tsuu, wait, wait."

Crane: "Goodbye, goodbye."

Still crying, the crane flew away into the sky. Circling over the house once, twice, three times, she flew away.

THE END